# To my Nanna.

Thank you for the love and lessons you give me.
Spending time with you is always fun.

Jeremiah is on his way to his nanna's house. He spends his days with her while his parents go to work. He is excited because today Nanna will take him to the barbershop. They arrive at Nanna's house and she greets him at the door with a warm hug and kiss. She then helps him out of his hat and coat so they could start their day.

First, they have breakfast. Jeremiah's favorite is
Nanna's grilled cheese sandwich and hot tea
with lemon. Once they are done with breakfast,
Nanna starts her morning cleaning.
Because she is in a wheelchair,
Jeremiah loves to be her little helper.

So she straps him into her wheelchair and up and down the room they go. He sweeps while she rolls the wheelchair. Next they dust the table and chairs and place the plates, forks, spoons, and butter knives on the mats. Before they settle down for a nap, they put a dinosaur puzzle together for fun.

Nanna likes to play jazz music as they get ready for their nap. She taps her feet and rocks Jeremiah back and forth in her wheelchair as he falls fast asleep.

After their nap, they get ready to put a pizza in the oven for lunch. Nanna shows him how to carefully place the pizza sheet pan into the oven.
She would always say, "Do not forget your oven mitts so the fire doesn't burn your fingertips."

After lunch they get dressed to go to the barbershop. Jeremiah loves to ride fast up the street in Nanna's wheelchair. Nanna explains to him they must be careful because they could get hurt if they do not wear their seat belt. He screams, "Faster, faster," as they fly down the street.

Mr. Nick is at the barbershop waiting for Jeremiah. As soon as he enters the shop, Jeremiah jumps into the chair and Mr. Nick begins to cut his hair. He likes it when Mr. Nick spins him around in the chair. "All done," says Mr. Nick. Jeremiah looks in the mirror and he likes his cut. He then hops back into Nanna's wheelchair so they could go to the store for some snacks.

On their way back home from the store, they enjoy the fresh breeze and wave hello to their neighbors as they pass by. Nanna says, "Soon your parents will be here to take you home, so let's get your belongings together." Jeremiah is excited to see his parents, but sad to leave Nanna.

To cheer him up, Nanna whispers in his ear,
"If you are good for your parents tonight,
we can race again in the wheelchair
tomorrow." Jeremiah was thrilled.

Soon Jeremiah's parents arrive to pick him up.
Nanna gives Jeremiah a kiss on the forehead
and waves goodbye. Jeremiah jumps for joy
as he gets into the car. He buckles his
seat belt as Nanna had taught him and thinks
about the fun he would have in the wheelchair.
He couldn't wait to return the next day.

**Jeremiah Alston is a** 9-year-old upcoming author. Before the outbreak of the coronavirus pandemic last year, he used to spend most of his time surrounded by a big family. The weekdays were always spent at his Nanna's house while his parents went to work. But the quality time spent with his family was cut short due to the pandemic. During this time, Jeremiah decided to put all his memories into short stories until he was able to spend time with his Nanna again. He hopes this book can help people around the world who maybe missing their loved ones. He keeps his memories of the fun he had with his Nanna in his heart until they can be together again.